THE SOD HOUSE

by Elizabeth Coatsworth

illustrated by Manning deV. Lee

Macmillan Publishing Co., Inc.
New York

With love for
Bill and Mabel

THE
SOD
HOUSE

More than a hundred years ago, a great many
people left Germany, because they were no
longer free to say what they thought. Among
these was a young man named Friedrich
Traubel with his wife, Maria, and their baby
daughter, Ilse. Friedrich had been brought
up on a farm, but as a boy, he was appren-
ticed to a cabinetmaker in Cologne. Later he
practiced his trade there.

"We will go to the New World," he told

his wife, Maria. "Little Ilse shall grow up in freedom."

"But the New World is very far away," said Maria timidly.

"I would cross ten oceans if freedom lay on the other side!" cried her husband, his blue eyes shining. Maria, seeing him so happy and so brave, took courage.

They crossed the Atlantic in a sailing ship, and settled in Boston. Soon Mr. Traubel rented a little shop where he made and sold fine furniture. The family lived in the rooms above the shop, and were very happy there. Ilse grew into a little girl with straight light brown hair, dreamy blue eyes, and a firm, sweet mouth that often smiled.

When Ilse was seven years old her baby brother, Hans, was born. Then the Traubels were happier than ever. But one winter Papa seemed very quiet. Often he lay awake until

6

late in the night. He no longer enjoyed the good dinners that Mama cooked for him. Even when Ilse climbed onto his lap in the evening for the good-night fairy story, he would sometimes forget what he was saying. He became silent, staring ahead of him, thinking thoughts which the others could not guess at.

At first Ilse would lean her head against his arm and look up into his face.

"Then, Papa, what did the prince do?"

But the happiness which had surrounded them was gone. The wonderful stories limped sadly, like lame horses. As the winter went on, Ilse learned not to disturb Papa when he was lost in his thoughts. Soberly she kissed him good night and went to bed.

Mama asked no questions. She was very quiet, too, and more gentle and affectionate than ever. One evening Mama was sitting by the lamp sewing, with baby Hans asleep in his cradle beside her. Ilse drew up her stool by her mother's feet and knitted a stocking. Suddenly, Papa began to speak.

"You know about slavery, Maria," he said slowly, "and you, too, little Ilse. There are no slaves any more here in the northern states where we live. But in the southern states, there are many Negroes who are owned just as horses and cattle are owned by a master. The fact that many of these masters are good to them makes no difference. It is wrong for any man to be the slave of any other man. It is bad for them both. Sometimes here in Boston, I feel my own freedom turn bitter, thinking about other men who are not free. Perhaps you do not know that in Congress there are more senators and congressmen from the South than from the North. Because of this they have things their own way.

But more free states are joining the Union. If the territory of Kansas becomes a free state, there will be more northern senators than southern ones, and then we can make a law setting the slaves free."

Ilse only partly understood what Papa had said but she could see that Papa was very serious. Mama stopped sewing, and now she said in a low voice, "What has it all to do with us, Friedrich?"

Papa reached over and patted her hand.

"Whenever there is an election in Kansas, gangs of men from Missouri cross the river and vote the southern ticket. A few stay on and take out claims. The only way we can out-vote them is for more people from the North to settle in Kansas than there are southerners."

Mama said hastily, "But you are a cabinet-maker, not a farmer, Friedrich!"

"I was a farm boy, before I was a cabinet-maker, Maria."

"But you have not savings enough to take such a long journey and to buy new land."

"No, I have not. But there are men who cannot go themselves, who will help us. They call themselves the New England Emigrant Aid Society. They buy land in Kansas. And they lend money to people from the North who wish to settle there. It is in this way that they fight against slavery. Today I talked with some of these gentlemen. They showed me maps. They have bought good land along the Osage River and this summer they plan to send out a dozen families to settle it. They will give us our share of the land, and help us beside."

Ilse got up from her stool, forgetting all about her knitting.

"Oh, Papa, shall we live in the country?"

Her father lifted her to his knee.

"Should you like to live in the country, Ilse? But you are a city girl."

"Yes, but I think I will like the country better."

"There, you see, Maria, little Ilse will go."

"And I will go. Didn't I cross the sea? But men can be more dangerous than waves. Is it a dangerous thing you are planning for us, Friedrich?"

"Yes, perhaps. But if we are doing God's will, we can come to no harm. Even if we die doing it, Maria."

"You are right, Friedrich." Mama quietly picked up her sewing again and bent her head over her work.

But Ilse sat happily in her father's lap, asking questions. And now at last Papa talked. All that he told her seemed like a wonderful fairy tale in which she would have a part. She could hardly wait for the days to pass. But at last the spring came, and Papa was ready. Everything had been sold except the clothes they needed and Papa's fine tools. Mama took some flower seeds and a young rose tree from the back yard, cut short and tied in a small burlap bundle. Papa took the old cuckoo clock which came from the German farmhouse where he was born, "for luck," he said. Ilse had a little doll, which her best friend, Marion Simms, who lived next door, gave her as a good-bye present. She was a penny doll, made of china. Her arms and

legs moved. She had black hair and black eyes and a little red mouth and was only three inches tall. Mrs. Simms dressed her in a little pink dress.

"She won't take up any room," Marion said when she gave Ilse the doll. " 'When this you see, remember me.' "

"I'll never, never forget you," Ilse promised. She sat the doll down on the palm of her hand. "Oh, I love her, Marion. Isn't she just like Thumbelina in the fairy tale?"

And from that moment Thumbelina was Ilse's constant companion. She carried her in her pocket while she helped Papa and Mama with all the bundles. Little Hans needed help, too, for he was still very little. When they were settled on the train, out came Thumbelina to see the passing wonders from the car windows. When the family ate their meals, Thumbelina had her crumb. And at night she slept in a fold of Ilse's coat, while Ilse curled up in the car seat.

On the second day on the train, Mama brought out her sewing bag and found a piece of rose-flowered cloth.

"What are you making, Mama?" Ilse asked.

"Little girls shouldn't ask questions," Mama said. But she was smiling. In a few minutes she had made a little bag, with a draw-string of pink ribbon.

"Here, Ilse," she said, hanging the beautiful little bag around Ilse's neck. "Keep Thumbelina in this when you carry her. She will be safer than in your pocket, where she might get broken."

At Iowa City the train went no further, and there they stayed for three days while Papa bought what was needed for the journey. He let Ilse come with him when he chose the wagon in which they would travel and

Big Peter and Little Peter, the gray horses.

"You'd better take the cow, too," said the dealer. "She's not much to look at and she's kind of bad-tempered. But the man from whom I bought the horses used her with them. Hereabouts they call a team of horses, with a cow pulling in front, a 'spike' team. She's a good leader. And she's a pretty good milker, too."

So Papa bought the old cow, whom he named Baldy, because her horns and the top of her head were white, while the rest of her was brown. The horses were handsome, but Baldy was a homely, thin cow, and Ilse felt sorry for her. She went to the side of the corral and picked some clover. When she took it to Baldy, the cow put down her head.

"Look out she doesn't hook you!" the dealer called, but Ilse just stood still, talking to Baldy. Soon the cow lifted up her head and

16

took the clover. Papa had been watching.

"Old Baldy will be in your charge, Ilse," he said.

When at last the wagon with its strong white canvas cover was fitted out and the horses harnessed to it, Baldy was harnessed in front, "to do her part, like everyone else," Papa said.

And the grim old cow understood her business as leader of a spike team. She walked along as fast as the horses, and kept the traces tight, pulling her share of the load. Papa and Mama sat on the wagon seat, with little Hans in Mama's lap. Sometimes Ilse stood behind them looking out between their shoulders. Sometimes she sat on the mattresses piled at the back of the wagon, looking out behind at the early spring landscape.

It was all so wide, so windy, so grassy. Ilse felt her heart grow big with joy. The days never seemed too long. Morning and evening, she loved to gather twigs for the cooking fires, and to wash and dry the dishes. Mama soon learned how to cook on a spider and how to bake in the Dutch oven which reflected the heat of the flames. In the evenings they would sit for a little while by the dying fire, watching the stars come out in the sky. Then they climbed into the safe wagon, where Mama and Ilse had made up the two beds. Meanwhile Papa brought in Big Peter and Little Peter and Baldy from grazing, and tied them to the wagon wheels, safe from thieves. Very early on the journey, Papa taught Ilse how to milk. Somehow, Baldy never kicked over the pail when Ilse milked. She would pretend to hook at her sometimes, and would pretend to kick out with the cow's quick side kick, but her horn or hoof never touched Ilse.

"Don't be naughty, Baldy," Ilse scolded, but she was not afraid of old Baldy. They were friends, and morning and evening she was proud to bring the pail of milk to Mama. She loved to hear little Hans laugh, as he reached out for the first tin cupful.

Thumbelina enjoyed all the journey. Ilse made sure that she saw everything. She showed her the dusty streets and straggling buildings of Nebraska City, and sat her on

the rail of the ferry when they crossed the yellow Missouri River.

"Now we are in Kansas," Papa said. That day the wagon tracks which they followed turned south.

"This is Kansas," Ilse told Thumbelina. "Oh, how many flowers there are, and so many meadow larks singing! I love it, I love it."

From Topeka they traveled south again,

and then a little east. One day they forded the Osage River and in the early afternoon came into Osawatomie, a town of one street of tents, log cabins and plank stores.

"Here we are," said Papa. "This will be where we get our supplies. I have a few things to buy, and I must ask directions to our land. We are almost home, Maria. Will you get out and stretch your legs?"

"No, Friedrich. Hanslein is asleep in my lap. Take Ilse and Thumbelina with you."

But when they went into the grocery and feed store, the tall, lank man at the counter stared at them with cold eyes.

Papa brought out a list, but the store-keeper did not glance at it.

"Where you from?" he demanded.

"Massachusetts," Papa replied.

"Who sent ye?"

"The New England Emigrant Aid Society."

"Thought as much. Well, let me give you some good advice. Get out and stay out, if you know what's good for you. You're not wanted here."

Something in the man's tone frightened Ilse. She held Thumbelina tight in her hand to keep her safe. What would Papa do? But Papa did nothing. He gave the man a long, steady look and then turned and without a word walked out into the sunlight. On the sidewalk a middle-aged woman in a sunbonnet was going by, and as she passed Ilse she said in a low voice,

"Tell your Pa Alvah Tuck will trade."

Ilse tugged at Papa's sleeve as he was about to climb back into the wagon.

"Alvah Tuck will trade, Papa," she said.

"Where did you hear that, Ilse? All right, we'll go along and see."

Alvah Tuck's shop was small and dark and

Alvah Tuck was a small dark man in his shirt-sleeves. There was a shotgun lying on the shelf behind him. He was glad to see Papa, and told him how to locate his land.

"You're lucky," he said. "The spring's on your property, I see. Thought twelve families were coming out?"

"There've been delays," Papa said. "I didn't wait."

"They were to have come last year and didn't. Hope you can hold out, way off there by yourself."

"You manage."

"Yes, I came three years ago, and I'm still here. But there aren't many of us northern men around these parts. Be careful."

He sold Papa salt and cornmeal and sweetening, small panes of glass to be set into windows, and some lumber which Papa said was green.

"It'll have to do," Papa said. But he chose some wood to be put aside to season, for making furniture later. "This I'm taking now is for the doors and temporary bedsteads. I'm a furniture maker by trade."

"Fine," said Alvah. "We need furniture. Right now there's scarcely five families of Free Soilers in the neighborhood, but we'll be a beginning."

Ilse noticed that Papa didn't tell Mama anything about why he hadn't traded at the first store. He talked about the furniture Alvah said people needed.

"But everything looks so poor, Friedrich," Mama answered. "It doesn't seem as if anyone had money here."

"There are other things beside money, Maria," Papa said. "I'd like to get a hen with a nice setting of eggs, or we could trade for a couple of lambs or a good pig. You wait and see."

Ilse sat down at her window in the canvas at the back of the wagon, watching the road unwind behind them. Suddenly she saw that they weren't alone. A man on horseback was following them, some distance behind. She waved to him but he didn't wave back.

"Perhaps he didn't see me," Ilse told Thumbelina. She waited until she saw the stranger looking directly at her. Then she waved again. But still he made no answer.

"Well, don't, then," she said to herself. But a queer little feeling came into her heart.

About four miles out of town they saw the spring below the road in a large sloping hollow, with a wooded gully leading down to the Osage River, about a mile away.

Papa drove onto the prairie and drew up, a little beyond the spring. As he helped Mama and little Hans down from the high wagon seat he kissed them.

"Welcome home," he said in a voice that Ilse had never heard him use before.

Then he lifted Ilse down and kissed her, too. She felt solemn and happy.

The prairie all about them was covered with tall grasses and flowers and the sun was low in the sky. The air felt cool and sweet. Together they went to the overflowing spring to drink, and Hans paddled his fingers in the clear water. Then Ilse led up Baldy, and Papa brought Big Peter and Little Peter and they, too, drank, and lifted their heads and drank again.

"Here we will build the house," said Papa. "Come, let us find wood, Ilse, and we will make a fire for the good Mama to cook us our first meal on our own land."

But before they ate, Papa suggested that they should sing "The Star-Spangled Banner." They stood side by side in the twilight,

Papa's big voice leading, and Mama's voice with Ilse's soaring up into the sky, like birds, Ilse thought.

There were red bars of sunset in the west and some long white clouds trailed above them. Far up in the soft blue sky the evening star shone,

"O'er the land of the free
And the home of the brave."

It was as if a great banner hung over them all. Ilse scarcely noticed that the rider who had followed their wagon from town was still there in the road, a motionless shadow against the sunset, lounging in his saddle, watching them.

For the next weeks they were very busy. At night they continued to sleep in the wagon's white canvas world, but all day they were out of doors. On a still morning Papa burned over a patch of prairie to make the work easier. Then he began to plow strips of sod with which to build the house.

When the high flowery grasses were gone, the Traubels saw that there were three or four mounds in the earth. Papa was careful to plow around these, as he said they might be Indian graves. One day when he was cutting sod near their camp, Mama and Ilse did the washing. Ilse brought the water from the spring to Mama's tub, and afterwards spread out the clothes on the clean grass to dry in the sun. When they were finished, they sat in the shade of the wagon, resting and playing with little Hans.

Suddenly Ilse saw something move in the tall grass near them, and an Indian stepped out. About his waist, he wore a leather belt and fringe, and he had on a necklace of bear's claws. A rifle lay across his thin arm.

As if he were alone on the prairie, he

walked past them without a glance, and down into the gully beyond. In a moment the eagle feathers in his hair mingled with the willow branches, and disappeared from sight.

Ilse pressed close to Mama and when she felt how Mama was trembling, she trembled, too.

"Shall I run and tell Papa?" she whispered. Mama shook her head.

"He's busy," she said. "We mustn't worry him." So Ilse said nothing. As the days went on and the Indian never came back, Ilse almost thought that he was part of one of the

stories she told Thumbelina when they were alone.

The sod house grew quickly, each strip of sod fitting closely upon the one below. At last the walls were well over their heads. Then Papa made a roof of willow branches from the gully and covered them over with a matting of dried grass. On top of this he put on a layer of sod, with the flowers and grass still growing from it.

"Oh, I hope a meadow lark will build her nest on our roof," Ilse said.

"Maybe one will some day, Ilse," Papa answered, smiling. "But it's too late this summer. The eggs are hatched by now."

Then Papa cut square openings in the walls for the windows, which he made with four little panes of glass in each. Next he built the heavy door, complaining sadly of the green wood. He was afraid it would warp in

the sun, he told Ilse. Whatever he was doing, she helped him, holding nails or bringing him the tool he needed, or brushing away the sawdust.

When at last the house was ready, she helped Mama bring in their furniture and put all to rights. Papa had made two temporary bedsteads. The wagon seat would be a bench and the table was only two boards laid across barrels with a red-and-white cloth on them. But the little stove was blackened until it shone, and the cuckoo clock hung on the wall as proudly as it used to hang in the house in Boston. Outside Mama planted her rose bush by the door.

The night when they had their first supper at their own table was a great occasion. So again they sang "The Star-Spangled Banner." After Hans was tucked safe in bed, Papa told Ilse stories in the dear old way, and she went

to sleep to dream of princes and elves. Once she woke up to hear the cuckoo calling out eleven times in the darkness. "Even when Papa builds a real house with shingles and wood from the sawmill, I shall love the sod house best," Ilse thought.

Now that the house was built, Papa built the barn with stalls for Big Peter and Little Peter and Baldy. The barn, too, had a strong door, which he could padlock at night, so that he knew the animals were safe from thieves as well as wolves.

Daytimes the horses were busy plowing for a late crop of sod corn and potatoes, but Baldy grazed all day and grew fat and placid. Every morning after milking, Ilse led her out a little way onto the prairie and staked her within sight of the house. Then to the comfortable sound of Baldy pulling at the green grass, Ilse played for a little while with

Thumbelina. Sometimes, she pretended that she was Thumbelina's size and put her head close to the ground where Thumbelina was sitting. Soon she began to see Thumbelina's world. The grasses were taller than church towers and among them hung the flowers, round and big as cart wheels. A lady bug was as large as a cat. She trembled when a rabbit hopped down a grass aisle. A prairie chicken running by, followed by her downy chicks, was bigger than the biggest elephant to Ilse, when she was in Thumbelina's world.

Other days, she would seat Thumbelina safely on a flower stem and let her sway there in the breeze, careful that she did not fall. Once she found a dead butterfly and made Thumbelina a cloak of its wings, as beautiful as anything a fairy princess ever wore. Ilse was so happy playing on the prairie that she didn't care when their neighbors from down the road sometimes rode or drove by without ever stopping to speak to them. Now, she no longer waved to them, even when there were children in the wagons.

But one day Papa came in for dinner looking especially happy.

"Maria," he said to Mama. "There are good people everywhere. Today a man was driving to town for supplies, and he pulled up his horses and called to me. Didn't you hear him?"

"No," said Mama. "Maybe I was churning

then and making too much noise to hear. But you bring good news, Friedrich. Do go on."

"Well," said Papa, his face bright with goodness. "This man gave me a sack of oats. He said last year he raised more oats than he could use, and he thought I might like to grain the horses after the day's work. 'Sod plowing's hard work,' he said. 'That's a nice looking team you have.' I thanked him and said did he know I didn't believe in slavery? 'Sure,' said he, 'but I don't ask what a man's politics are. It's enough for me that he's a neighbor.' "

Mama's eyes were shining. "Everything will be all right!" she said. "Perhaps this good man's wife may come to see us. And perhaps they may have little children, too."

"I shall give the horses some oats this evening for a treat," said Papa.

That night Ilse was wakened by the sudden

scratch of a match. Something was wrong in the barn and while Papa lighted a lantern and ran out, Mama and Ilse got the stove going and put on water to heat.

All night Papa worked to save Big Peter and Little Peter, but he only saved Little Peter.

The oats which the man had given him were poisoned.

Ilse did not cry when she knew that Big Peter was dead. She was too unhappy to cry. She had not dreamed that such things could happen. After that, when a rider or wagon went by from down the road, she turned away her head and ran into the house and shut the door. She did not want to hear even the sound of their wheels.

One day Papa followed her into the house and sat down and took her into his arms.

"Don't hate them, Little Ilse," he said. "If

you hate them, they will succeed, for they will have made you bad, too. Think how afraid a man must be to do a wicked thing like that."

And Ilse tried to think how afraid the man had been, but still she could not look up when the neighbors went by.

Now Baldy's lazy days were over and she plowed with Little Peter and grew thin and bad-tempered to everyone but Ilse. Papa and Mama went quietly about their work, but Papa didn't whistle anymore, and Mama didn't hum. Ilse thought that Thumbelina had grown quieter.

Then one late afternoon when Papa had finished his work and come into the house, three men rode up to the doorstep and called out his name. Mama tried to hold him back, but Papa opened the door and went out.

"Good evening, neighbors," he said

quietly. The three men had guns hung to their saddle bows and they didn't say "good evening."

The oldest of the men had a long gray beard.

"We want to get this straight," he said. "Are you for slavery or are you against it?"

Papa smiled at him.

"I am against it," he said.

"That's all we want to know!" one of the younger men shouted. "What are we waiting for, Uncle Jed?"

"Look behind you, Jim," said the older man.

Ilse had hidden her face in Mama's skirt, but when she heard the man say "Look behind you," she peeked out and saw seven Indians on ponies in a ring behind the three men. Their unshod horses had come through the grass almost without a sound. Now the

Indians just sat there. Five of them had guns across their knees. They were waiting.

When the man called Jim saw what was behind him, he didn't say anything more. But the older man spoke once again.

"This is our last warning," he said, and lifting his reins, rode away, followed by the two younger men.

Father thanked the Indians and asked them to come into the house and eat.

"The one on the spotted horse is the one we saw, Mama," Ilse whispered.

Mama nodded.

But the Indians said they had far to go.
They made Papa understand that the day
before one of them had overheard the neighbors when they made their plans to drive
Papa off his land.

"But why are you my friends?" Papa asked,
looking at them gratefully.

The Indian on the spotted horse pointed towards the mounds.

"You don't plow our graves."

"But no one would!" Papa exclaimed.

"THEY do."

Ilse had an idea and whispered it to Mama.

"Yes, Ilse, it can do no harm," Mama said.

So Ilse ran off with the milking pail to where Baldy was tied, nearby on the prairie. In a few minutes she brought the pail back half filled with foaming milk, and carried it shyly to the Indians with a tin cup.

The Indians didn't bother about the cup, but passed the pail from hand to hand and drank it all, until each had his mouth ringed with white foam. Then they lifted their right hands in a gesture of farewell and disappeared down the gully.

"But suppose they hadn't got here?" Mama asked. "What will happen next time?"

"Next time may never come," Papa said cheerfully.

The days went on, and in spite of her fear of the neighbors, they were happy days for Ilse. Their little house had so much sky over its flowering roof and such wide prairies all about it! Papa had finished planting the corn and potatoes in the sod furrows, and now he made a small garden behind the house. Then he smoothed the inside of their big room with clay and whitewashed it.

"This is like home now," Mama said, and brought out from the chest some curtains which they had used in Boston. She had to cut them in half to fit the little windows. One day Papa drove them all into Osawatomie and brought back the seasoned posts and planks to start making furniture. And he even bought a strip of carpet to lay on the hard earth floor.

As they drove home Mama kept speaking of the carpet.

"Such foolishness," she said softly.

But Papa said, "I want you to be happy here, Maria."

Mama smiled at him. But she could not say that she was happy, even with a rose-flowered carpet. It was Ilse who laid her cheek against Papa's arm and said, "I am happy, Papa."

"Yes, you bloom here, Ilse. Your cheeks are like roses."

"What delays the others? If only they would come, I, too, would be happy," Mama said. "It is for you that I am always afraid, Friedrich."

"But we are in God's hands, Maria."

Ilse scarcely heard what they said. She was thinking that the road was golden like a road in a fairy tale, for sunflowers grew in a yellow bank on each side, curving across the prairie to their little house with flowers on its roof.

Several times they went to the Osage River to fish, and took their lunch to eat in the pretty wooded valley through which the river ran. They saw deer under the trees and new kinds of flowers. It was pleasant for a change to have green leaves over their heads, instead of the wide sky. But Ilse loved the sky best. Mama and Hans rode on Little Peter, with Papa guiding him by the halter, and Ilse followed, leading Baldy. After Big Peter's death they were afraid to leave any animal behind.

Day after peaceful day went by. They saw nothing of their neighbors, except for some thin line of smoke from a far-off chimney, or a passing wagon or a rider trotting by. Sometimes then Little Peter would raise his head and whinny, for he was lonely without Big Peter. The passing horses might whinny back an answer. But the only greeting was between the animals.

One hot afternoon when the wind was blowing from the south, Ilse was puzzled to see that a black cloud was coming up over the curving horizon of the prairie.

"There's going to be rain," she called to Papa and Mama, who were inside the house. Papa came to the door to look.

The cloud was very black and it was moving fast. Already it was towering above the prairie, and the sunlit grass and flowers seemed very bright against it.

A rabbit came bounding past the house, never glancing at them. Another followed. Then a flock of birds flew by, uttering cries of alarm.

The black cloud was whirling upwards as it approached. Mama came to the door.

"I smell smoke, Friedrich!" she cried.

"You are right, Maria! The prairie's on fire!" Papa said. "Close the doors and windows while I get Little Peter! We'll be safe by the river."

That day Little Peter was picketed to one side of the house by himself. Papa ran and brought him back, snorting and fidgeting. It was hard to keep him still long enough to get Mama on his back. When Papa lifted Hans into her arms, Little Peter jumped and Hans hit his head against her shoulder and began to cry. Papa swung Ilse up behind Mama.

"Hold tight, Ilse," he said and they were

off, Papa running by Little Peter's side, holding the halter. The horse kept throwing up his head, trying to free himself from Papa's hand. He snorted and plunged so that Papa had all he could do not to be thrown off his feet and trampled. Hans was frightened and his head hurt. He bawled and struggled in Mama's arms. It was hard for her to hold him.

And just then Ilse, looking backwards, saw Baldy. The cow was trying to pull her picket chain loose, but she could not budge it. She was mooing and her eyes rolled. Ilse could not leave her there to die. Papa had always said that she must take care of Baldy.

"I'm getting Baldy," she called to Mama, as she slipped from Little Peter's back. But Mama, trying to quiet the struggling Hans and to keep her seat at the same time, never heard her, nor felt her hands loosen from her waist. Papa did not see her, either.

Alone across the prairie Ilse ran. The black cloud towered above her like one of the wicked genii. Now below it she could see the red of running flames, and the howling of the wind was mixed with the cries of the birds flying before it. A big rabbit struck against her legs and nearly knocked her over, but she ran on.

By the time she had unfastened Baldy, it was too late to reach the river. They were cut off by a wall of fire. The sun was darkened, and ashes were blowing about them. But Ilse did not lose her head. She must get Baldy into the sod barn at least, and Baldy, too, was glad to seek shelter in the stall that had always meant safety to her.

Panting in the darkness of the windowless building, Ilse looked about. Only the door would burn. If she could wet it down, now! The spring was not far off.

She snatched a horse blanket from the peg on which it hung. There were no pails in the barn as the animals were taken to the spring to drink, but a wet blanket would not burn easily. Closing the door behind her to keep Baldy in, Ilse ran stumbling towards the spring. All about her tongues of flames, torn loose by the wind from the roaring fire which followed, were flying by her. The air was hard to breathe.

She reached the spring and wet the blanket. But now it weighed so much that she could scarcely drag it after her. Still, she did not give up easily. She was stumbling over the sod now, and the dry grass with which it bristled was catching fire here and there about her. The great wall of flame was rushing down upon her. Already it was splitting about and engulfing the barn as a fiery river might split about and engulf a boulder. The sod house, too, was surrounded by fire. She was lost.

But even now Ilse kept her head. The heavy wet blanket dragged at her arms, as though reminding her that it was there. It was her only hope. Spreading it out on the furrowed sod, she crawled under it, making herself as small as she could. Her chest pressed against the ground, and she felt something hard and small against it.

"Are you all right, Thumbelina?" she whispered and she thought she heard Thumbelina whisper back, "I'm all right."

Then the roaring filled her ears, and a great something crawled over her across the wet blanket, making a sizzling sound, and in a moment had passed by. She heard the uproar of the fire racing on and on across the prairie, driven by the wind. Further and further off it sounded, and at last she dared

lift up the steaming blanket. She was not
hurt. All about her the ground lay black, with
here and there a wisp of smoke curling up
from it, or a feeble tongue of fire dying as she
watched it. The grass and flowers were
burned from the sod roofs of the house and
barn, but the buildings were standing. Even
the smoke-blackened windows in the house
were not broken, but the doors were smoul-
dering.

Now she could walk across the ashes. When Papa and Mama hurried back they found Ilse hard at work with the milking pail, throwing water against the house door. She had already put out the fire eating at the barn door. She looked black as a chimney sweep.

"Baldy's safe!" she called to them. "And Thumbelina's all right, too!"

Papa and Mama did not scold Ilse for the fright she had given them when at the river they found that she was not with them. They listened to her story and knew how well she had done her duty.

"A miss is as good as a mile," said Papa. "The fire never came down into the river bottoms at all. Thanks to you and the fact that the doors were made of green wood and didn't catch fire easily, no harm has been done, except to the garden, and we can plant that again."

"But harm was intended, Friedrich," said Mama wearily. "The people down the road set the fire to burn us out."

"Then they didn't succeed," said Papa cheerfully. "We must heat water for Ilse. She needs a bath. And so does Thumbelina."

Papa might be cheerful, but Mama could not shake off her sadness.

"We are in God's hands," Papa comforted her.

But now everything frightened Mama, and when two days later some covered wagons stopped on the road above, she tried to keep Papa from going to the door.

But he kissed her and said, "Be of good heart, dear Maria," and went out on the door-step.

"Can we camp here by your spring?" the driver of the first wagon called.

"Anyone is welcome to use a spring," Papa answered.

Slowly the wagons filed down from the road and drew up on the blackened prairie near the water. Ilse counted eight wagons in all and there were women and children in them, as well as men.

Standing with Mama and Hans at the window, Ilse saw a little girl near one of the wagons with a kitten in her arms. And a woman was leading a white goat to drink. She wanted to run out to talk with them, but Mama laid her hand on her shoulder and her hand was trembling.

"More of them," she said in a low voice. "They don't know who we are yet. When they know—." Papa, too, said nothing, but stood in silence by the open door, watching. Soon the man who had called to him walked up.

"Mr. Traubel?" he asked pleasantly, extending his hand.

Papa shook hands with him.

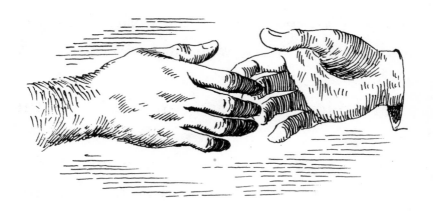

"How did you know my name?" he asked.

"They told us in Boston that you had come on ahead."

So here were the Emigrant Aid people at last, after they had almost given up hope of their coming! Ilse might talk to any of them. She might pet the kitten and pat the goat and show the children Thumbelina and tell the story of her doll's adventures.

Mama began to sing again as she tidied her hair at the little mirror before going calling. So many questions to ask and answer! All the ladies wanted to see Mama's sod house. Soon she was making tea for them and laughing and chatting as they sat on the edges of the beds and the bench and Mama's chair, drinking tea out of tin cups and Mama's two pretty china ones.

Their claims lay all about the Traubels' land. Counting the big boys, there were

eleven men, too many for those others down the road to want to make trouble with.

That evening after a happy supper, Papa and Mama sat on their doorstep looking down at the encampment a little below them. Over the shadowy earth, the sky was pale green and very clear, and the wagons seemed like a village of small white houses. Hans was asleep in Mama's arms and Papa drew Ilse on to his lap. In contented silence, they watched the people moving about their supper fires.

"It is good to have neighbors again," said Papa. "We have come to a good land. And some day we shall have friends all about us."

Ilse leaned her head against his big shoulder. Excitement had made her drowsy.

"Will THEY be friends? Even those down the road?" she asked, sleepily.

"Some day they will be friends, too," Papa promised.

AFTER

WORD

Today we should call the years of struggle in Kansas a cold war. The control of the territory was vital to both the North and South, for whoever held Kansas would hold the majority in Congress. Settlers were brought from Alabama as well as from New England, but the climate favored northerners, who were used to snow and ice. For the families from the Deep South, one Kansas winter was as much as they could face. The next spring most of them went home. This was of course less true of the determined fighters who moved in from Missouri, Kentucky and Texas. The battle for control was long and hard-fought, and only when at last the South had lost it, did she resort to open arms.

The Indian who watched from the grasses as Mr. Traubel plowed around the graves may well have been the man named Monday Blackhoof, who could have recited Wordsworth's poem which begins "I wandered lonely as a cloud," and might even have quoted a little Latin from "Julius Caesar." He was, I believe, an Osage, and had spent five years at the Shawnee Mission School under the Reverend Mr. Thomas Johnson. But he liked neither the school nor its principal. How gladly he had returned to his tribe, and the rolling earth and the wide sky! Still, he might have told the Traubels that Mr. Johnson, as a young man riding across eastern Kansas, had brought with him, from Kentucky, saddlebags filled with bluegrass seed, which he scattered on either side of him as he rode along.

Much of the grass in which Ilse played had come from Mr. Johnson's bluegrass seed. But Monday Blackhoof did not like Mr. Johnson, so he said nothing about it.